Happy Birthday, Brayden!
Dec. 19, 2010
G'ma loves you!
xx ooxx

Happy Birthday, Brayden!
Dec. 19, 2010
G'ma loves you!
xx oo xx

Birdie Halleluyah!

Judith Kerr

Collins

An Imprint of HarperCollinsPublishers

For Daisy and Millie Perrin

This edition first published in Great Britain by HarperCollins Publishers Ltd in 1998

1 3 5 7 9 10 8 6 4 2
ISBN: 0 00 198316 4

Text and illustrations copyright © Judith Kerr 1998

Printed and bound in Singapore by Imago

His real name's a secret,
but I call him...

"BIRDIE

HALLELUYAH!

He looks after me...

...most of the time.

Sometimes he forgets,

or he's busy,

or his mind is on other things.

But he's usually there when it matters.

Sometimes I wish he'd go away
because he can be quite bossy.

But it's good that he's there
at night when it's dark.

I don't know what he does while I'm asleep.
I suppose he goes home to see his friends.

And they do things together.

They probably have a very good time.

He's always there in the morning

and sometimes he brings things back.